LIVING WITH
DINOSAURS

by Patricia Lauber

illustrated by Douglas Henderson

Bradbury Press / New York

Collier Macmillan Canada / Toronto
Maxwell Macmillan International Publishing Group / New York • Oxford • Singapore • Sydney

The author would like to thank Dr. Donald Baird, Director
Emeritus of the Museum of Natural History at Princeton University,
for his thoughtful comments and generous help.

Bradbury Press
Macmillan Publishing Company
866 Third Avenue, New York, NY 10022

Collier Macmillan Canada, Inc.
1200 Eglinton Avenue East, Suite 200, Don Mills, Ontario M3C 3N1

FIRST EDITION
Printed in the United States of America
1 2 3 4 5 6 7 8 9 10

Library of Congress Cataloging-in-Publication Data
Lauber, Patricia.
Living with dinosaurs / by Patricia Lauber ; illustrated by
Douglas Henderson. — 1st ed.
p. cm.
Includes index.
Summary: Recreates life among the dinosaurs living in North
America seventy-five million years ago.
ISBN 0-02-754521-0
1. Dinosaurs—North America—Juvenile literature.
{1. Dinosaurs.} I. Henderson, Douglas, ill. II. Title.
QE862.D5L457 1991
567.9'1—dc20 90-43265 CIP AC

To illustrate *Living with Dinosaurs*, Douglas Henderson created 26 new full-color pieces, using a variety of media including pastels and gouache. In addition, the author and artist decided to include Douglas Henderson's pictures shown on pages 25, 32, 34, 42 (right), 43, and 44, from the collection of the Museum of the Rockies, in Bozeman, Montana; and illustrations on pages 35, 36, and 42 (left), from the artist's personal collection.

Cover: Shore birds, pterosaurs, and gigantic crocodiles were a few of the animals that shared the world of dinosaurs some 75 million years ago. *Title page:* A pterosaur flies through a forest of the lowlands.

The text of this book is set in 16 point Garamond No. 3.
Book design by Christy Hale

Contents

1. Sea, Shore, and Sky

Picture yourself going back through time—back some 75 million years to the days of dinosaurs. The place where you find yourself is now part of Montana. But it does not look like the Montana we know. For one thing, it is on the western shore of a warm, shallow sea. The sea stretches from the Gulf of Mexico to the Arctic, and it cuts North America in two. You are standing on the shore of that sea.

Earlier in the day, around dawn, mist rose gently from the sea, tinged pink by the rising sun. Now the mist has burned off and the day promises to be clear and hot. The air is salty, soft, and slightly damp. It smells like seashores everywhere.

Sometimes dinosaurs come down to the sea, to look around or graze on plants that grow behind the beach. They may also feed on plants growing in the shallow waters between the shore and some nearby islands. But they never swim out to sea. Dinosaurs are not sea-going animals. Right now there are no dinosaurs in sight, but both sea and sky are full of life. The world of dinosaurs is shared by many other kinds of animals.

Flying reptiles, *Pteranodon,* soar and glide above the shore of the inland sea.

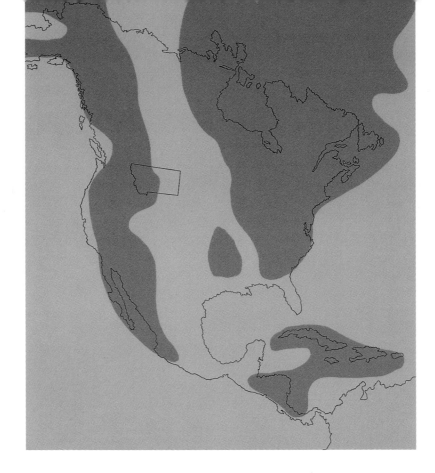

On this map present-day North America and Montana are shown in outline. The land masses of 75 million years ago are shown in brown, separated by the waters of a shallow sea.

Overhead, patches of sky are dark with wings. Some are the wings of seabirds, flapping, soaring, gliding. Like today's birds, these have feathers. Unlike them, these have teeth, which they use in snatching fish from the sea.

Most of the wings belong to another kind of animal. They are long and narrow and made of skin that is covered with thin hair. These are the wings of flying reptiles, of pterosaurs. Pterosaurs appeared on earth at about the same time that the dinosaurs did and are related to them. Over the years there have been many sorts and sizes of pterosaurs. The smallest have the wingspans of sparrows. Before the pterosaurs die out along with the dinosaurs, some will be as big as small airplanes, with wingspans of 40 feet.

The biggest pterosaur flying over the inland sea is *Pteranodon*. Like all reptiles, it grows throughout its life—older adults may have a wingspan of 23 feet. *Pteranodon* has a short body and hardly any tail. At the end of its neck is a small head with a huge crest and a big bill. Smaller pterosaurs have teeth, which they use to catch fish. *Pteranodon* does not. Perhaps it feeds like a pelican, scooping up fish and swallowing them whole. Perhaps it fishes in shallow waters, like today's long-legged herons, standing on one leg and snapping up fish and other creatures of the sea.

On land pterosaurs walk like birds, but they must run to build up speed for take-off. Once in the air, the smaller pterosaurs flap their wings, glide, and soar. *Pteranodon* does little flapping because of its size. For this big creature, flapping flight takes huge amounts of energy. *Pteranodon* spends most of

Pteranodon is the biggest pterosaur of the inland sea, with a wingspan of up to 23 feet.

its time soaring on rising currents of air. It soars and glides, swoops down, then rises again to soar above sea and shore.

Near one of the islands there is a sudden movement. A six-foot-long bird has popped to the surface. This is *Hesperornis*, a bird that cannot fly or walk. When a female must go ashore to lay her eggs, she lies on her belly and pushes herself along, as if she were sledding on the beach. It is a slow and clumsy way to move. But in the water, the birds are swift, skilled swimmers. At the surface, they sail along, kicking with their large webbed feet. To look for food, a bird flattens its tiny, stubby wings against its sides and dives. It will chase any fast-moving fish it sees, grasping the prey with its sharp teeth.

Smaller pterosaurs are hunting for fish in the same waters as *Hesperornis*, birds that cannot walk or fly.

Among the animals of the sea are turtles, squid, and fishes. The turtle is
Archelon, which may grow to a length of 12 feet and is a powerful swimmer.
Because it has weak jaws and no teeth, it eats only soft foods, such as
jellyfish. The fish, *Xiphactinus*, is about 13 feet long. It can eat another fish
nearly half its own length.

Beneath the surface of the sea, many kinds of animals are
going about their business, feeding or trying to escape becom-
ing a meal for some other animal. Crabs scuttle across the sea
floor. Snails graze on sea plants. Fishes flit everywhere. Some are
sucking up tiny plants and animals from the sea floor. Some are
nibbling on bigger plants. Others are looking for clams,
shrimp, and small fish. Not far away, a shark swims lazily,
looking around, perhaps not hungry.

The warm sea is also home to a number of reptiles. Only one looks familiar, a big sea turtle. The rest are animals no longer seen on earth.

Among these reptiles are the mosasaurs, relatives of today's monitor lizards. They look something like toothed whales. The smallest kind of mosasaur is 7 to 20 feet long, with a slim body and a fringed tail. It lives near the surface of the sea, paddling with its flipper-like legs and sometimes making shallow dives for food. It eats fish—and is itself sometimes eaten by other mosasaurs and sharks.

A middle-sized mosasaur is about 24 feet long, with a thick body. Its tail is as long as its body and flattened from side to side. It glides through the water like a snake, with S-shaped movements of its body, and steers with its stubby legs and webbed feet. It makes deep dives to hunt, catching fish and other soft-bodied creatures. It can also use its strong jaws and teeth to crack open shelled animals such as ammonites. It is sometimes attacked by a shark but may fight back well enough to escape being eaten.

Some mosasaurs are giants, growing to a length of about 40 feet. They are fearsome creatures. Like their relatives, they have huge appetites. Their enormous jaws let them catch and eat large prey—small mosasaurs, sharks, *Hesperornis*. Able to dive deep, they also feed on giant squid 27 feet long. Like other mosasaurs, they swallow their prey whole and headfirst, the way today's snakes and lizards swallow theirs.

A small kind of mosasaur swims near a big seaweed called kelp and shelled animals known as ammonites.

Another big reptile of the inland sea looks like a cross between a snake and a turtle, with a thick body and a long, slender neck. This is a plesiosaur. It swims by flapping its four huge flippers as if they were wings. When hunting, the plesiosaur may swim near the surface, raise its long neck, and look around. As soon as it spots a fish or squid, its long neck plunges into the sea and its sharp teeth close on the prey.

Plesiosaurs must beware of some of their relatives, the pliosaurs. About 20 feet long, a pliosaur has a streamlined body, a short neck, and a huge head with powerful jaws and strong teeth. Using its front and back flippers like wings, a pliosaur shoots through the water when chasing prey. It attacks and eats large fish and squid. It can also overcome a shark—or a plesiosaur.

Although the sea is their home, all these reptiles must come to the surface to breathe. They cannot take oxygen from the water, as fishes do. Sometimes they come to the surface, breathe, and dive again. Other times they float near the surface, with their eyes and nostrils just above the water.

Some kinds of sea reptiles may give birth to live young in the sea. The young swim quickly to the surface to breathe. There they become prey for fish and other animals, unless they can hide in beds of seaweed.

A plesiosaur swims near a large shark,
which is apparently not hungry.

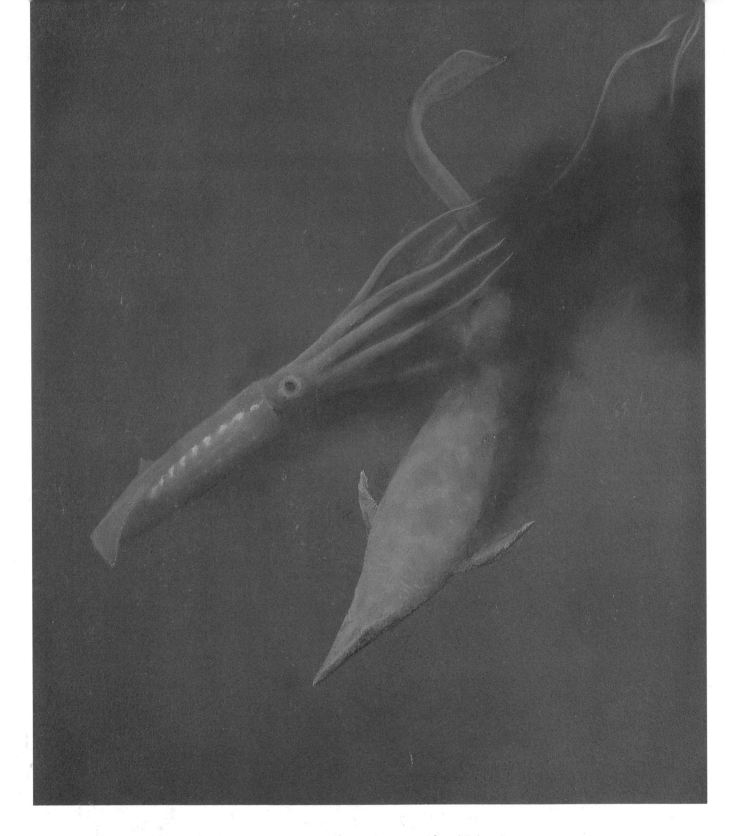

Above: A giant mosasaur attacks a giant squid, which tries to escape
by shooting out a blob of inky black liquid that will confuse its enemy.
Right: Two *Hesperornis* head for the surface near a pliosaur.

Other reptiles of the sea lay eggs, and they must go ashore. The females haul themselves out of the water onto beaches. With their short legs, sea turtles are clumsy and slow on land. The other reptiles are even more clumsy, because they cannot walk. They must squirm and wriggle, hauling and pushing with their paddle-like legs to reach the places where they will dig their nests. The trip is a time of great danger, when the reptiles are easily preyed on by land animals. Land animals also eat reptile eggs, if they can find them, as well as newly hatched young making the long trip down the beach to the sea.

The meat-eaters come from the low-lying land beyond the shore.

A mosasaur hauls herself up the beach to lay her eggs, while seabirds hunt for food, such as the sawfish that has been washed up from the sea.

2. Swamps and Forests of the Lowlands

You leave the beach, where seabirds and small pterosaurs are squabbling over crabs they have found. As you move inland, the sound of the quarreling dies away. You enter a forest, where the light is dim and the trees shade you from the sun's hot rays. You hear the rustling of leaves and the buzzing of insects. Somewhere something is chomping on leaves and twigs. You hear grunts and honks and the crash of heavy footsteps.

You have entered the lowlands of a plain that borders the inland sea. The plain reaches 250 miles westward. Here in the lowlands it is a world of green, thick with plants. It is a world of forests, freshwater ponds, streams and rivers, swamps, and inlets where rivers and sea meet and mix. In this world of water and greenery, many kinds of dinosaurs and other animals make their homes. There is space to live and plenty of food for animals that eat plants—and for animals that prey on other animals.

The freshwater ponds are home to fishes, frogs, and turtles. In one of them, a frog floats on a water plant and has just caught a fly. Beside the pond duck-billed dinosaurs are feeding. Standing

In the green lowlands, rivers meet the sea and their waters mix.

on all fours, they are browsing on cycads, which look something like palm trees. They also eat pine needles, magnolia leaves, and fruits and seeds. Like all duckbills, these have a broad, flat snout with a beak that looks like a duck's bill. The beak has no teeth, but the back part of a duckbill's mouth is lined with rows of teeth for grinding up plant food. As old teeth wear out, new ones grow in.

These dinosaurs are *Corythosaurus.* They belong to the group of duckbills with crests on their heads. *Corythosaurus* has a fan-shaped, hollow crest. When one of them calls to another, it makes a booming noise, like a foghorn, with the help of its hollow crest.

One corythosaur seems to hear something. It stands on its hind legs, ready to run. It listens for a short time, then decides all is well. It drops back to all fours and goes on eating.

These crested duckbills are big animals. They are 20 to 40 feet long and weigh as much as 5 tons. But like all plant-eaters, they must be on guard against meat-eaters. There are several kinds of tyrannosaurs around.

One is *Daspletosaurus,* which has short, deep jaws armed with large teeth. Each tooth is curved, with a dagger-sharp point and edges like saws. Attacking, it uses its teeth, its clawed hind feet, and the 4-ton weight of its great body. Hiding among trees and leaping out with gaping jaws, *Daspletosaurus* can overcome duckbills and even the horned dinosaurs.

Small herds of horned dinosaurs roam the forests of the lowlands. In some of these forests, palms, cycads, and ferns grow beneath tall strands of cypress, pine, and sequoia. In others, closer to the sea, there are trees that look like today's sycamores and beeches. Magnolia, dogwood, and poplar also

Beside a pond three corythosaurs find cycads, pine needles, and magnolia
leaves to eat.

Daspletosaurus attacks with teeth, claws, and the weight of its heavy body.

grow in the forests. The horned dinosaurs browse on low-growing trees and shrubs, as well as ferns and cycads. They can eat the toughest of plants with their powerful jaws and sharp beaks.

Some of the horned dinosaurs have as many as three horns, which they use as weapons against tyrannosaurs. Their necks are protected by a huge sheet of bone, called a frill, which grows from the back of the skull and curves upward.

Styracosaurus has a huge, straight horn on its nose and two smaller horns above its eyes. Its neck frill is armed with spikes. Seen head-on, *Styracosaurus* is a terrifying sight. If it is attacked anyway, it lowers its head and charges.

Plant-eating styracosaurs have a fearsome appearance, with three horns and a spiked neck frill.

Chasmosaurus has an even bigger frill that covers its neck and upper shoulders. The frill is edged with bony knobs and spikes. The dinosaur uses its frill to warn off other dinosaurs, but it can also defend itself with the horns of its nose and brow.

Some horned dinosaurs are quite small, and not all of them have horns, in spite of their name. *Leptoceratops* is one of these. It is 7 feet long and much more lightly built than many of its relatives. It moves about easily on two legs or all four, and its hind legs are built for running. If attacked, it tries to escape by speeding away. *Leptoceratops* can use its front feet as hands, grasping leaves with its five clawed fingers and stuffing them into its mouth.

Horned dinosaurs, such as *Chasmosaurus,* attack enemies by charging with their heads down. Sometimes two males fight over a female.

Leptoceratops has no horns or neck frill, but the bones at the back of its skull form a peak.

When dinosaurs walk, there is no mistaking their heavy footsteps. But the smaller animals of the forest move with quick, light steps, marked by the rustle of leaves or the snap of a twig. Many are lizards, darting from one hiding place to another. Others are mammals, furry animals that nurse their young on milk. All the mammals are small, only inches long.

One kind looks something like today's opossums, and it is good at climbing trees. Another looks more like a shrew. The

A mammal scurries through the litter of the forest floor, through ferns and the leaves of such trees as magnolia, sassafras, and sycamore.

Ornithomimus walks on a fern-covered forest floor, hunting food.

mammals eat insects and other small animals, fruits, seeds. They do not compete with the dinosaurs for food or living space. But there are small dinosaurs that eat mammals.

One of these is *Ornithomimus,* an 11-foot dinosaur that looks like an ostrich. It has a small head with large eyes and a horny beak, like a bird's. *Ornithomimus* eats fruit, leaves, insects, lizards, and mammals. It catches and grasps its food with its long, clawed fingers. It may also eat the eggs of other dinosaurs, dashing away at speeds of 30 miles an hour if caught in the act.

A herd of *Kritosaurus*, which are duckbills without crests, crosses a river near the sea, keeping nostrils and eyes above water. The fish, like today's gar, is a fierce hunter with sharp, pointed teeth.

There is a path through the forest, beaten down by the feet of dinosaurs. It leads to a river, where the animals go to drink. The land near the river is swampy and smells of rotting plants. The air is hot and sticky.

The river is wide here. On a sandbar in its middle, two tyrannosaurs, *Albertosaurus*, are standing over a duck-billed dinosaur that they have brought down and killed. When they have eaten their fill, the remains will become food for other animals, some of them as small as flies and beetles.

On the bank of the river, a gigantic crocodile dozes in the sun. It has nothing to fear from *Albertosaurus*. Its body is armored with a thick hide and scales. Its great jaws and huge sharp teeth are its weapons. With them it can bring down a large dinosaur and drag it into the water to drown. Most of the time, though, the crocodile eats fish and turtles and smaller land animals that make the mistake of coming too close to its jaws.

The sun is well overhead now. It's time to move on, to follow the river westward, to visit the uplands of the plain.

Two albertosaurs stand over a duckbill they have brought down.

3. The Upland Nesting Grounds

The sea is a hundred or more miles behind you now. The greenery of the lowlands has also been left behind. As you travel westward, the land rises gently. Overhead the sky is a clear blue bowl and the sun is a blaze of light. The air is hot and dry and sometimes dusty when a welcome breeze sweeps the ground.

Rivers flow across the upland plain, twisting and turning in wide curves. There are also streams that come together to form a river. Other small streams will flow into rivers farther east, in the land behind you. You see a number of shallow lakes that will dry up later in the year.

Something about the plain looks strange. This kind of land ought to be covered by grasses, but there are none to be seen. The reason is that there is no grass anywhere on earth. It has not yet developed. Instead, the land is either bare or covered with thickets of berry bushes. Other plants hug the banks of streams, rivers, and lakes. There are dogwoods, evergreens, the big palm-like cycads, and still more berry bushes.

In the uplands, streams come together and form rivers. The light haze is caused by ash and dust from a volcano.

31

Although the uplands are generally dry, at certain times of year they are drenched by monsoon rains that cause widespread flooding.

Several kinds of dinosaurs live here in the uplands. Among them are duckbills, hypsilophodonts, and horned dinosaurs, all of which feed on trees and bushes. There is also *Albertosaurus,* as well as some smaller meat-eaters. Fish and turtles live in the rivers. And if you look sharp you will see lizards and some tiny mammals.

The duckbill munching on a berry bush is *Maiasaura,* a duckbill with a flat head and no crest.

When the time comes to lay eggs, *Maiasaura* females gather in colonies. Each builds a nest, piling up mud in a big mound, 10 feet in diameter. She makes a hollow in the middle, where she lays her eggs in circles. The nests are spaced out. The distance

During the dry season *Maiasaura* females arrive at their nesting grounds and make their nests. They are being lightly dusted by volcanic ash.

Varanid lizards make a lightning-quick raid on a *Maiasaura* nest. They are the largest land lizards.

between one nest and another is about 25 feet, the length of a female's body. Once her eggs are laid, a female covers them with leaves and other plant materials. As the plant parts rot, they give off heat, which warms the eggs.

The females wander off to feed on dogwoods and evergreens, but much of their time is spent standing, sitting, or lying down near their nests. They are on guard against lizards, small dinosaurs, and other animals that would like to eat the eggs.

The newly hatched young of *Maiasaura* are not ready to take care of themselves. They stay in the nest, scrambling over one another and waiting for their mothers to bring them food. The females are very busy now, coming and going, their small heads bobbing on the end of their long necks. Once they have fed themselves, they gather berries and other food, which they store in their cheeks and carry back to the young. When the wind blows toward you, you learn that the nesting ground is a smelly place. It is also noisy with the cries of hungry young and the loud honks of adults calling out to their young.

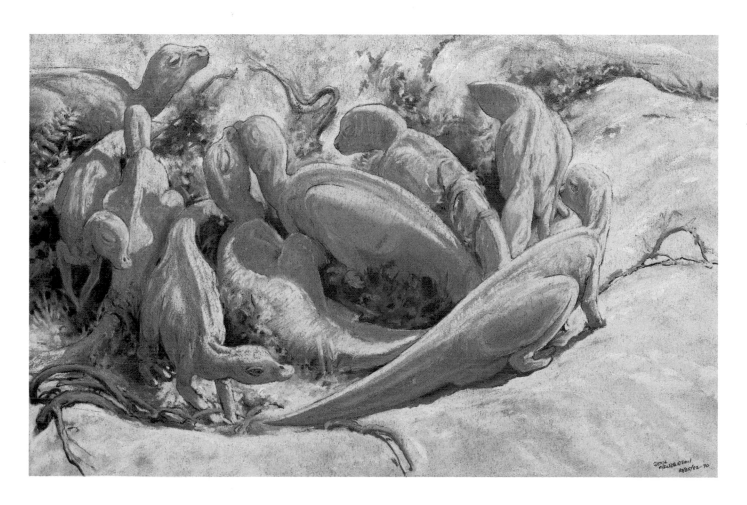

For the first month or two of their lives, *Maiasaura* young stay in their nests and are fed by their parents.

When the young do leave their nests, they stay with their mothers. They learn to find food and eat it. In time they are ready to move on with their mothers and other duckbills to new feeding grounds.

A shallow lake lies near the *Maiasaura* nesting grounds. In it is a small island, thick with plants—small trees or bushes and sedges, which look like grasses but have hollow stems. From the shore it's hard to see any animals. The plant life is too thick. But animals are there. The island is a place where *Orodromeus,* a kind of hypsilophodont, come to lay their eggs.

A small island in a lake is the nesting grounds for *Orodromeus.*

Adult *Orodromeus* tend their nests on the island.

Hypsilophodonts are small, quick, graceful dinosaurs, about 7 feet long. They travel in herds, feeding on plants. If attacked, they try to escape by running away on their long legs.

Each year when the lake is high, the females arrive to lay their eggs. They do not make nests but lay their eggs in mud. Each female lays about 24 eggs and covers them with plant material. Young *Orodromeus* hatch out ready to take care of themselves. They can walk and run and find their own food on the island.

Although it is hard to see the hypsilophodonts, other animals know they are there. Albertosaurs cross over to the island. So do the small meat-eaters known as *Troodon,* which snatch eggs and young. Lizards also steal eggs. Beetles and other insects feed on fluids left in the eggs after hatching and perhaps on eggs that did not hatch. Mammals feed on the insects and may be eaten by lizards.

Troodon, like other meat-eaters, is likely to raid the *Orodromeus* nesting ground and make off with some hatchlings.

The sun is low in the sky now. Soon it will set behind the mountains at the western edge of the uplands. There a great change is taking place in the earth. The Rocky Mountains are being born. Sometimes as they are thrust up, earthquakes shake the land. Volcanoes erupt and the sky turns black with clouds of smoke and dust and ash. Here and there you can see a faint coating of ash on plant leaves. Puffed out by a volcano, it drifted through the air and fell to earth. A shadow sweeps across the land. It is the shadow of a pterosaur, flying back to its nest in the lowlands. Night is coming.

It is time to go, to leave the world of dinosaurs and return to the present.

To the west the Rocky Mountains are being thrust up.

Digging up the Past: How We Know What We Know

No human being ever saw a live dinosaur. No one ever saw a pterosaur, a mosasaur, or most of the other animals in this book. All died out about 65 million years ago, long before there were people to see them, remember them, and tell of them. Yet today artists can draw pictures of them and writers can write books about them. To do so, artists and writers use the findings of scientists who study remains and traces of long-ago animals and plants that are preserved in rock.

The traces can be bones or whole skeletons, footprints, teeth, shells, eggs, burrows, tree trunks, prints of leaves. Together all these remains and traces are called fossils.

Most living things do not become fossils when they die. Instead, they slowly disappear. Their soft parts rot away, and their hard parts are worn away by wind and water. But sometimes a plant or animal is preserved because it is quickly buried. It may become a fossil.

Long-buried fossils tell us of earth's past. Here the scientist who was uncovering the skull of an albertosaur in Montana decided to finish his work later when a bear appeared at the site.

How a Fossil Forms and

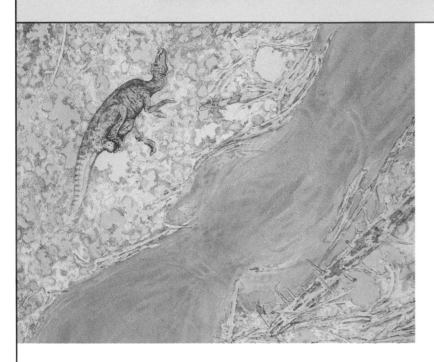

Suppose a duckbill dies in a swamp near a river. Its body settles into the swamp and the soft parts start to rot away. Water flowing slowly through the swamp keeps dropping tiny bits of soil and rock—sediments—that it is carrying. The sediments build up on top of the dinosaur, burying it deeper and deeper. Sometimes, after heavy rains, the river jumps its banks. It drops still more sediments. After a while, the soft parts of the duckbill disappear. But the hard parts, the bones and teeth, are left, buried under layers of sediment. A print of the skin may also be left.

The sediments go on building up. The weight of new layers presses down on the old. Minerals in water may act as glue, binding the sediments together. After a long time has passed, the old layers become rock. Sealed inside that rock is a fossil—the bones of a duckbill. The bones themselves may be changed by minerals from the water, which make them harder. Minerals may even take the place of the materials the bones were made of. The bones become rocks that are shaped exactly like the bones. They too are called fossils.

Later Comes to Light

Over millions of years the climate and the landscape change. Now sediments are no longer building up. Instead, they are worn away by wind and water. The layers of soil and rock above the duckbill grow thinner and thinner.

In time they are worn away entirely, and the duckbill fossil comes to light. It too will wear away unless it is found and collected. If it is, scientists may study it to learn about the past.

Volcanoes can also play a part in the forming of fossils. When the Rockies were growing, volcanoes often erupted. Blasts of hot gasses swept the uplands, killing the animals in their path. Thick layers of ash buried them. Mudflows from the volcanoes clogged lakes and rivers, sending their waters surging across the land. The bones were buried under ash and mud.

Fossils tell scientists about animals no longer seen on earth. They tell about plants that grew millions of years ago. When plants and animals are found in the same layers of rock, scientists know that they lived at the same time.

Plant fossils are clues to climate. Palm trees and cycads, for example, tell of a warm climate. They show that Montana in the days of dinosaurs was much warmer than it is now. The lowlands were probably much like the coast of Louisiana today.

Fossil teeth are clues to what animals ate. Sharp teeth, suited to tearing and cutting, are the sign of a meat-eater. Wide, blunt teeth tell of an animal that ate tough plant food. Smaller, narrower teeth show that the owner ate ferns, mosses, and other soft plant foods.

Sometimes an animal died soon after it had eaten another animal. If the animal became a fossil, so did its meal. That is how scientists discovered that giant mosasaurs had giant appetites and ate other mosasaurs, as well as sharks and *Hesperornis*.

While studying the fossil of a smaller mosasaur, they found that a shark had tried to eat it. In its spine was the broken-off tooth of a large shark. The spine showed that the mosasaur had healed— that it had escaped and lived. Toothmarks on the shells of ammonites show that they were among the foods that mosasaurs ate.

By studying fossils, scientists have learned what the earth was like during the days of dinosaurs. They have learned how animals moved around, what they did, what they ate. They have learned which animals lived at the same time.

The days of dinosaurs lasted 140 million years. During that long time, many great changes took place on earth. When the first dinosaurs appeared, the earth had one huge continent, which was surrounded by one huge ocean. Later the giant continent broke in two. Still later the two continents broke up. Pieces of them drifted over the surface of the earth and became the continents we know today.

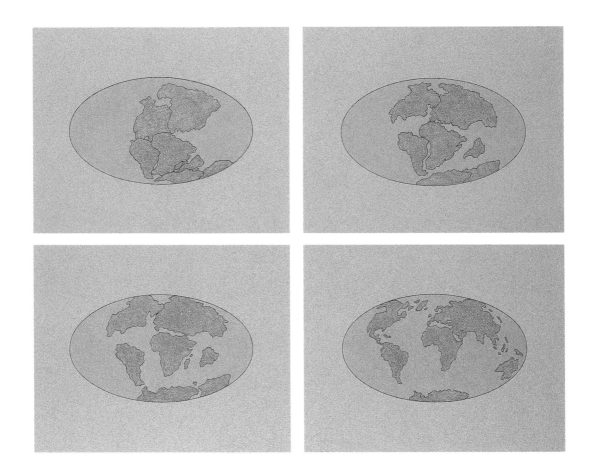

Early in the days of dinosaurs, the earth had one big land mass. This continent first broke in two, then into smaller pieces that became the lands we know today.

Meanwhile, new oceans opened up. Inland seas appeared—or disappeared. Old mountains wore down and new mountains were thrust skyward.

While all these changes were going on, many kinds of dinosaurs developed and later died out. But the dinosaurs were never the only animals on earth. Their world was always shared by many other kinds of animals. These competed with one another for food and living space. And on land they had somehow to live with dinosaurs.

Dinosaurs were the rulers of the land. They took for themselves the living space and food that they needed. There was room and food only for animals that could use what the dinosaurs were not using.

The dinosaurs died out at a time when the earth's climate was cooling. In the middle of North America, land was rising and the inland sea drained away into the Gulf of Mexico. When the sea disappeared, so did its plants and animals. In a cooler, drier climate, land life changed. Some plants died out. Others did better in a cooler climate and these spread. The changes affected animals that ate plants—and animals that ate animals that ate plants.

Some animals lived through these changes. Among them were the mammals. For them the changes meant a world in which dinosaurs no longer ruled the land. For them, scientists say, the changes offered a chance to grow in numbers and size and to spread out. New kinds developed and went on developing. The time had come for mammals to rule the land. So it is perhaps just as well for us that the dinosaurs died out, for we are mammals too.

But by using our brains, we can learn about worlds that existed long before people did. By using our imaginations, we can go back 75 million years, look around, and see the dinosaurs and their world. We can hear the wind in the trees of ancient forests, feel the warmth of the sun, and sniff the salt air of a vanished sea that covered what is now the Great Plains.

Index and Pronunciations

Illustration references are in **boldface type**.